Thank You!

From the bottom of our hearts at the Wise Womb Foundation, we are grateful for your purchase. Wise Womb is a 501(c)(3) tax exempt organization and profits go to fund our mission. We strive to prevent the rising conditions in women's health today like endometriosis, PCOS, PMDD, painful periods, infertility, and traumatic birth experiences with education to empower women to make informed health decisions. To combat the maternal and infant mortality rates in NYC, we fundraise to provide certified, culturally sensitive doulas to mammas in underserved communities during live births.

Thank you for supporting our commitment to educate females about women's anatomy, cycles, and childbirth. We hope these pages leave you feeling empowered and knowledgeable.

We encourage all communication. Follow us for more information.

With Love,

Olivia, Julie, Adele

Co-Founders of Wise Womb Foundation

Table of Contents

Wise Womb Foundation

A preventative approach for the future of women's health

Established in NYC 2024

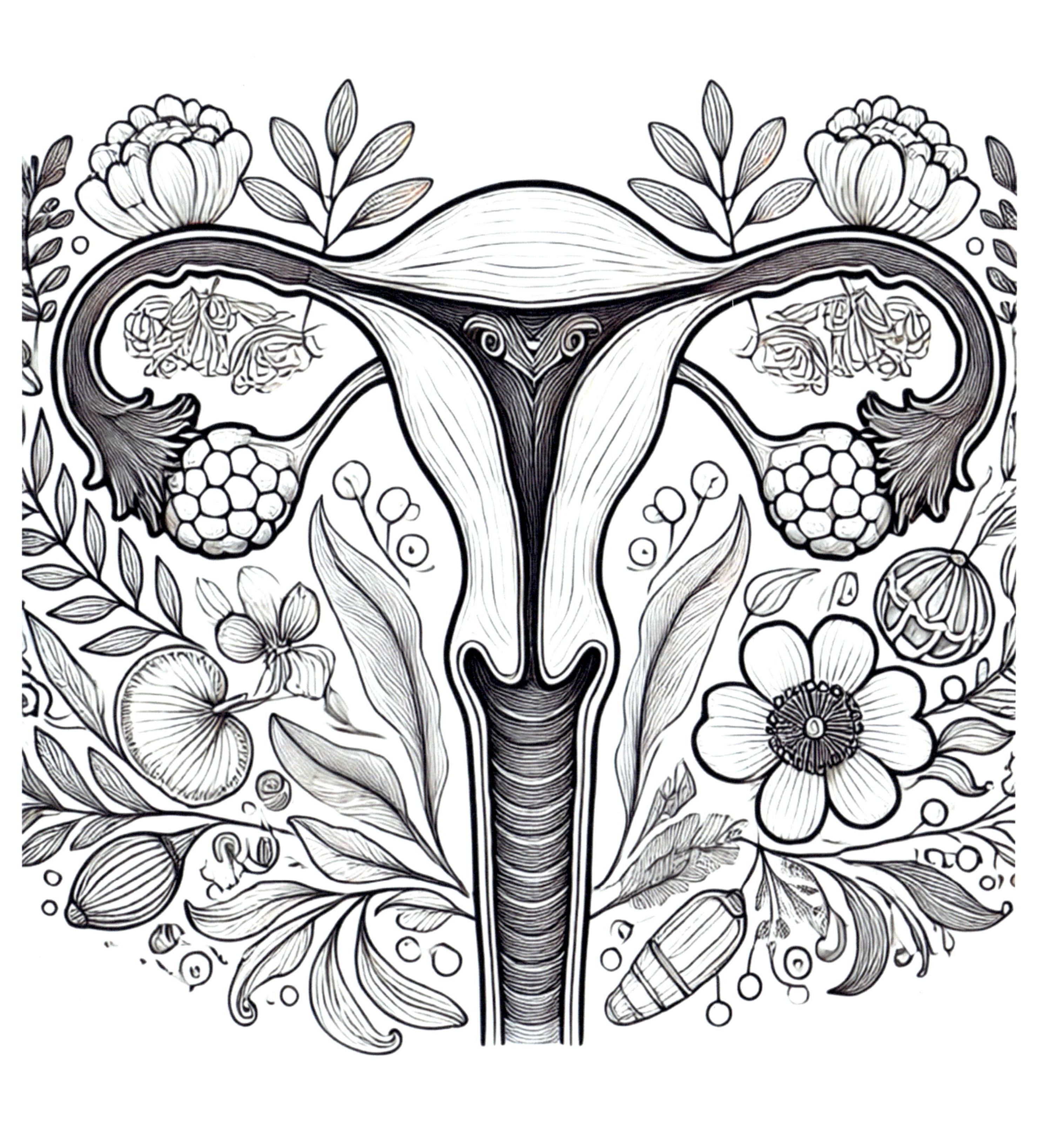

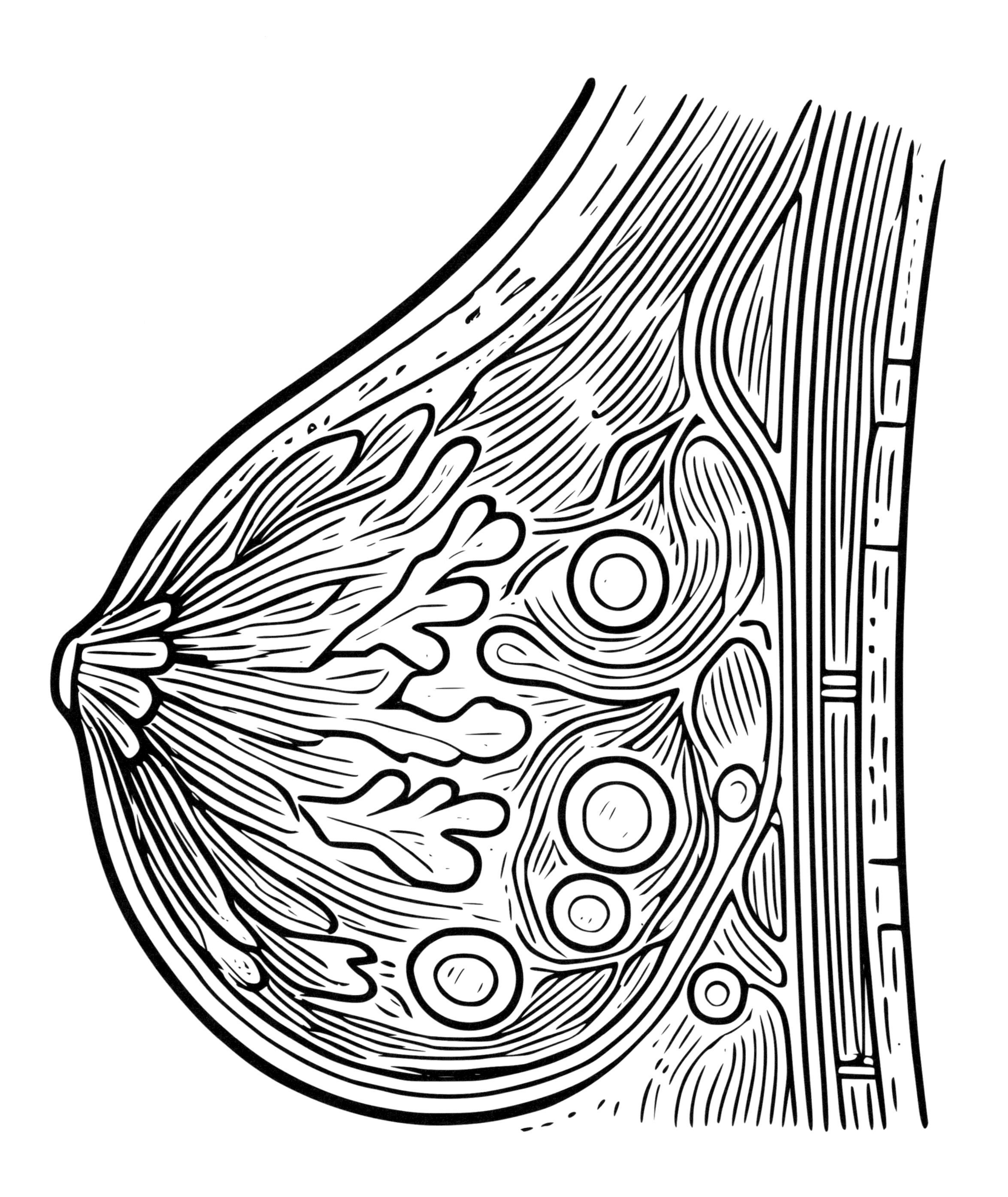

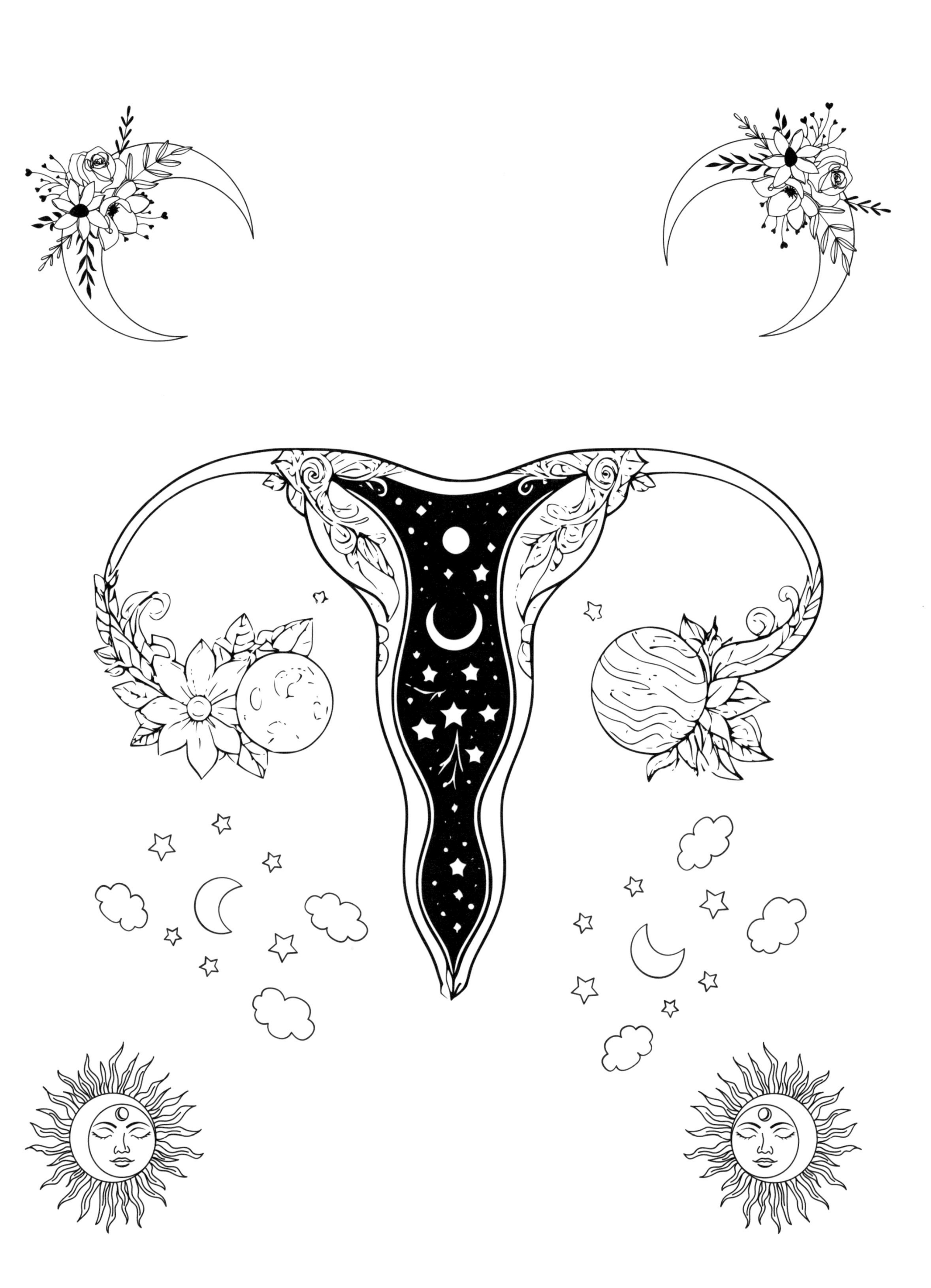

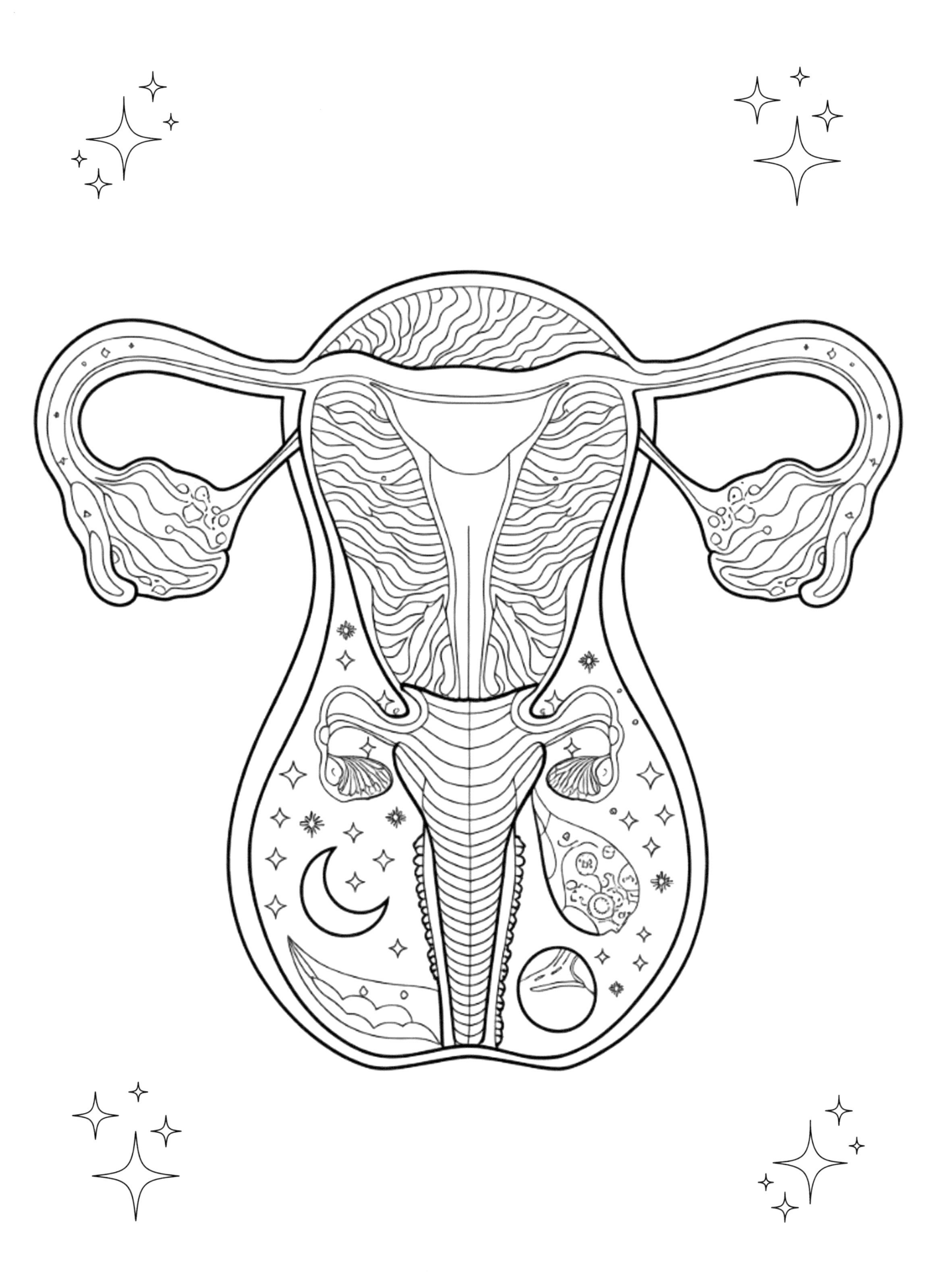

Female Anatomy

Words Matter

Vulva versus Vagina : What is the Difference?

Vulva refers to the external surface of the woman's genitals, including the outer and inner labias, clitoral hood, and opening to the inner canal, a.k.a. the vagina. The vagina is the muscular canal that goes from the uterus, through the cervix, down to the outside of the body. The majority of people miscall the vulva, vagina, which underscores our lack of knowledge about the woman's body.

What does 'Yoni' mean?

Yoni is a word in Sanskrit that translates most closely to mean 'womb,' 'sacred temple,' or 'source.' In Hinduism, Yoni represents our innate power as women, referred to as 'Shakti' in Sanskrit. It means beyond the physical organs of the uterus, vagina, and vulva, it refers to the Divine Feminine spirit.

What is a G-Zone and does the G-spot exist?

There is no such thing as pressing a button, or hitting the g-spot, to turn a woman on. However, approximately 2 inches inside on the front wall of the vagina, along the pubic bone, there is a sponge of erectile tissue that is coined a G-Zone. This area can become engorged during arousal. If this area has been neglected, the tissue could be desensitized and shriveled up. Incorporate resensitization practices (later in the book) to build neuropathways and circulate blood to this area to experience pleasure and g-spot orgasms.

Watch our Womb Anatomy Class in the Wise Womb Library

Female Reproductive System

What parts make up the female reproductive system?

The major organs that make up the female reproductive system include the uterus, where implantation occurs and a fetus grows, fallopian tubes that receive ovaries, ovaries that produce eggs and hormones, cervix that opens to allow blood to flow during menstruation and birth to occur, and vagina which is a canal that connects the uterus to the outside of the woman's body. Even though this image represents the female reproductive system, in the body the ovaries hang down.

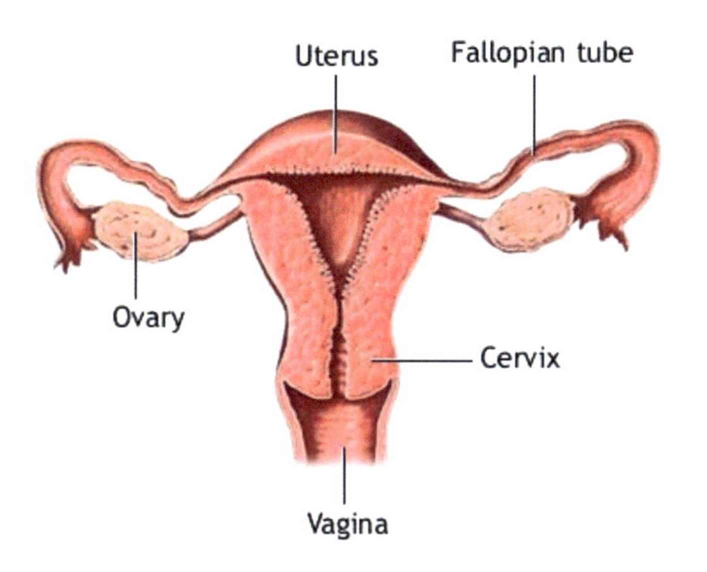

Female Reproductive System

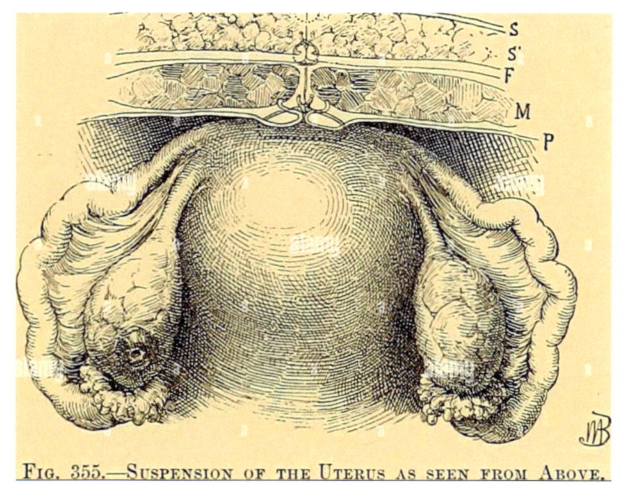

Fig. 355.—Suspension of the Uterus as seen from Above.

Anatomical diagram of ovaries in female

Female Genitalia Anatomy

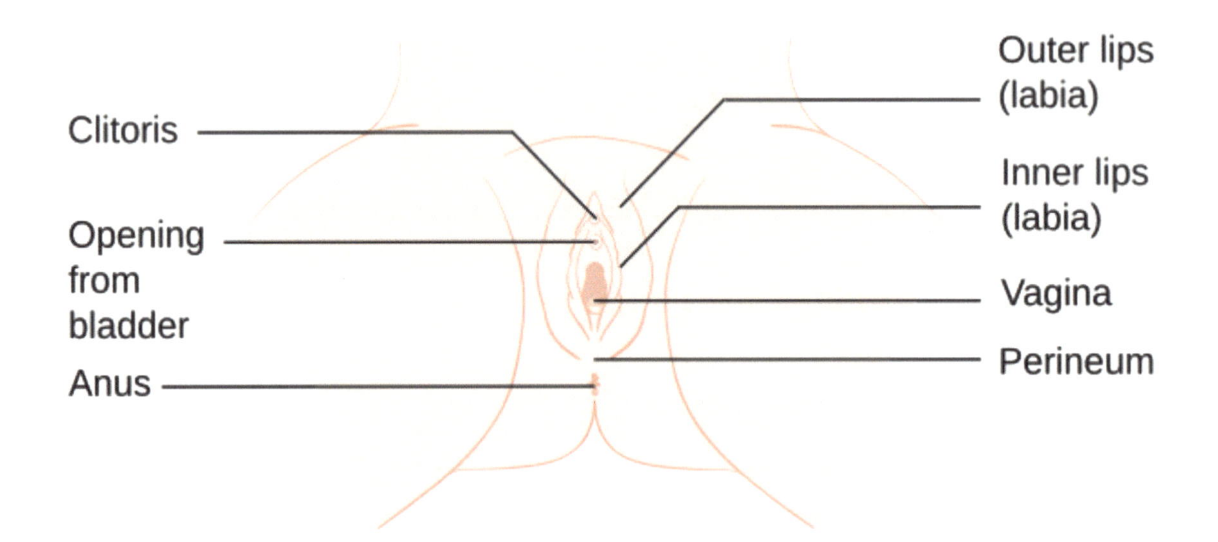

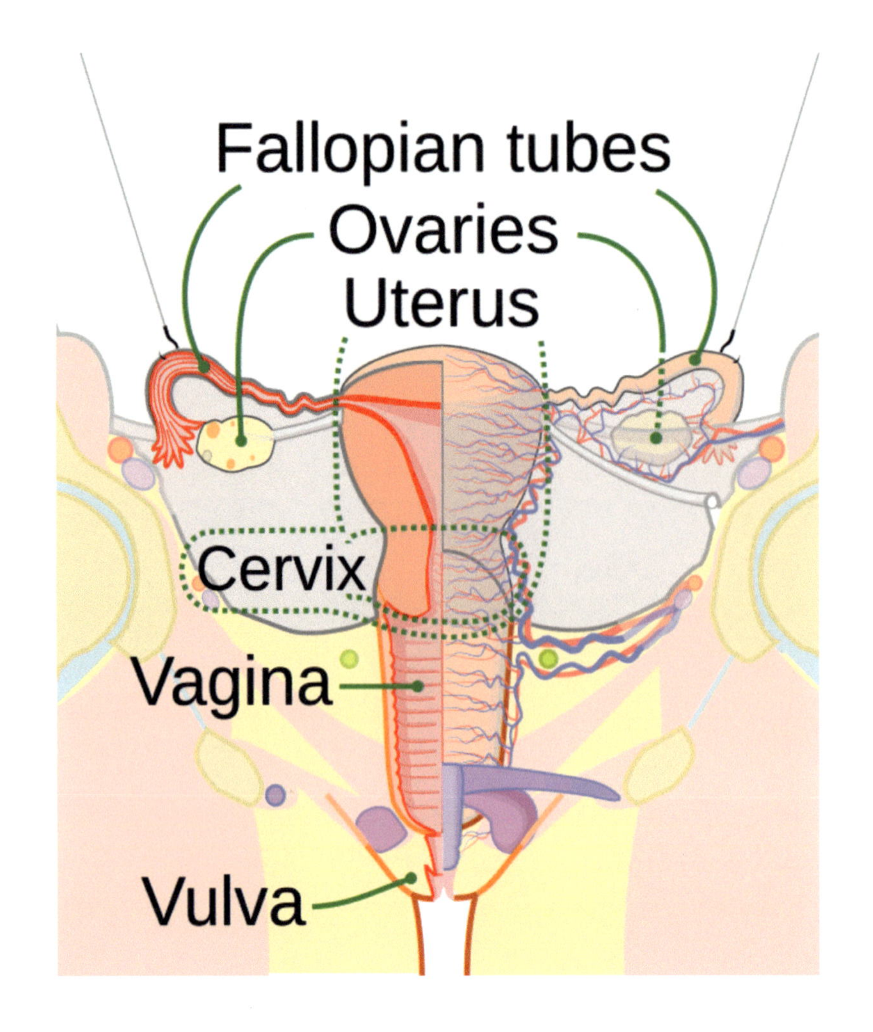

Clitoris

What is a clitoris and what does it look like?

A clitoris is an organ in the female reproductive system that becomes erect from arousal. Its sole function is to make a woman feel pleasure during intimacy. It is the only organ in male and female bodies designed for pleasure only, even a male penis is simultaneously used to excrete urine. It is much more than the visible 'crown jewel' we see externally. She has glands and legs behind our outer vulva lips and inner vulva lips.

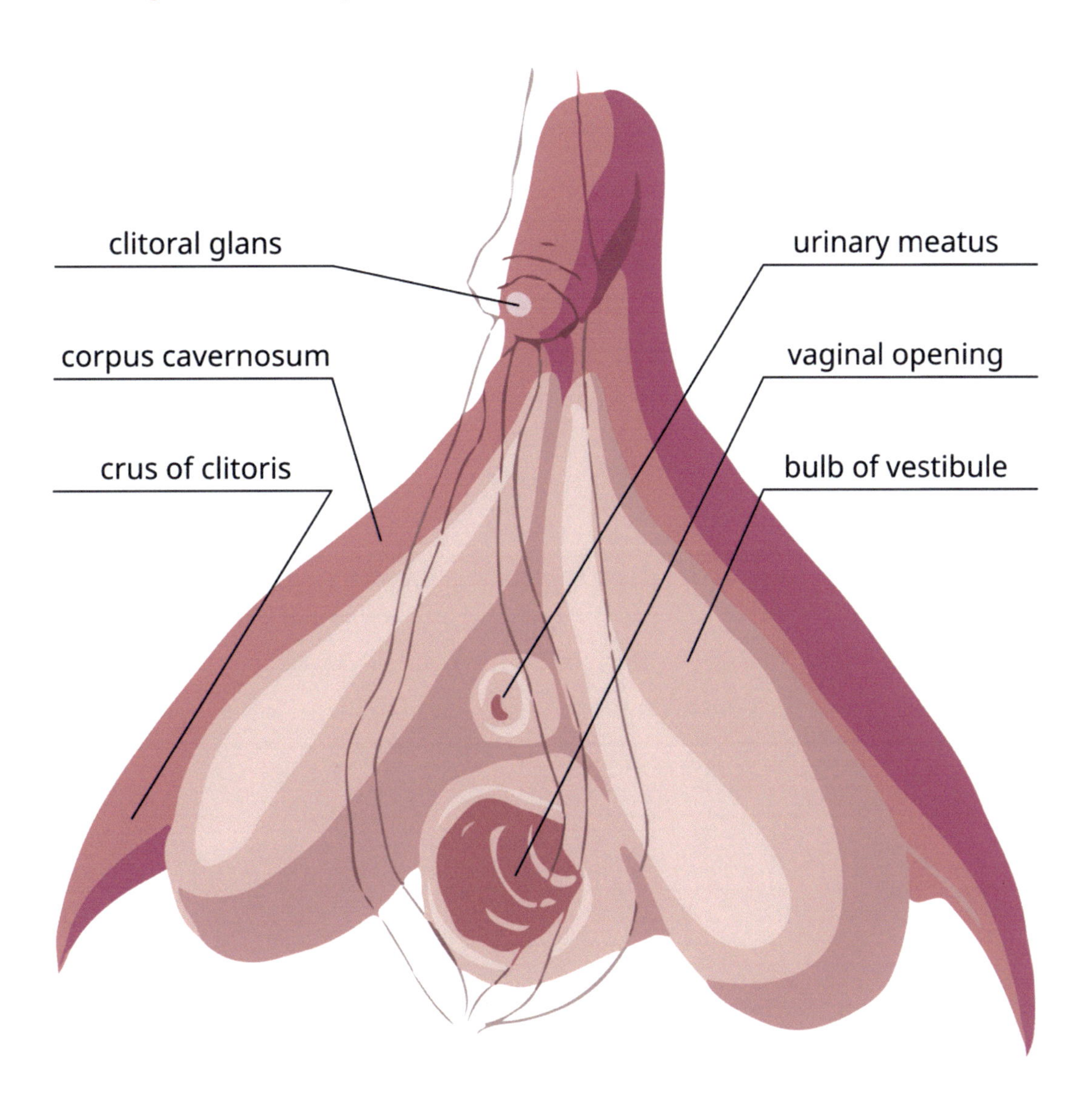

Recall Time

Label these parts:

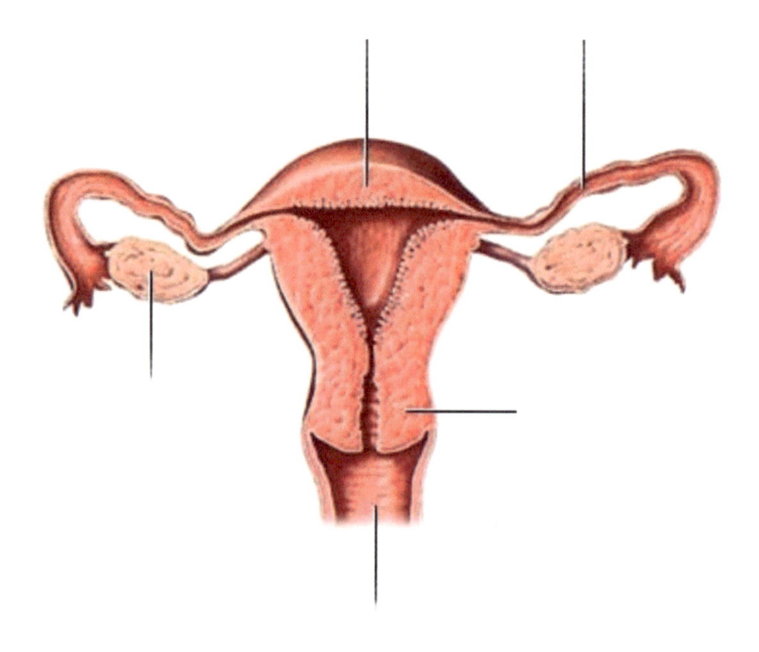

What does a vulva refer to?

____

____

____

____

____

Practices to Connect to Your Vulva

Practices to Connect to Your Vulva

Exploring your own body with love and softness is the most empowering thing you can do for yourself as a woman.

Intimate Gazing

Use a hand mirror and prop your back up comfortably against pillows. Take time to look into your portal of life. Breathe. Gently observe and be compassionate.

Cupping

Place your palm over the opening of your vulva and hold your Yoni. Take a deep breathe in, expanding your belly, and exhale through the mouth making a sound.

Yoni Steams

Pour ~20 oz boiling water over 2 tbspn of a blend of organic herbs such as calendula, rose, lavender, chamomile, or others into a bowl and wait a few minutes. Squat over it and let the steam rise into the womb.

Sacred Rituals

Prepare an altar in honor of Her with fresh or dried flowers, shells, candles, crystals like moonstones & carnelian, mirrors, bowls of water, feathers, and symbols that ignite passion and love.

Yoni Steam

Yoni steaming is a feminine practice found across diverse cultures such as India, Greece, eastern Europe, the Philippines, and Japan. There is evidence in the ancient world about the use of Yoni steams.

From the Trotula in 12th century Salerno, Italy, it writes, "*Afterward we make a fumigation for females which in a marvelous manner is effective and strengthens. Take clove, spikenard, calamite storax, and nutmeg, and let them be placed in an eggshell upon a few hot coals. And let there be prepared a perforated chair so that all the fumes go toward the inside...We give it to drink, but we do not omit the above mentioned fumigation, which strengthens cold wombs.*"

Yoni steaming was practiced in the Mayan culture, which viewed womb care as essential as brushing teeth. It was incorporated into the La Cuarantena, or the 40 days Postpartum. It is referred to as *bajos* meaning 'down low.' Spanish friars documented these remedies from the Mayans and Aztecs. In Ancient Egypt, yoni steams were similarly used post-birth to cleanse and purify the uterus.

Indigenous people, including the Yoruba of Nigeria and the Zulu of South Africa, conduct yoni steams to celebrate the divine feminine. It is a spiritual practice that cherishes the oneness of woman, mother earth, and spirit. It is accompanied typically by a ritual with prayers, calling upon ancestors and nature spirits for healing.

In Korean culture this practice is called *chai-yok*. Aryuveda refers to the practice as *yoni swedana.* Traditionally it included mugwort, wormwood, and yarrow.

In Ancient Greece, "The Greeks called this continuous tube the hodos, the "road" through the body, and believed that in women whose genital tubes had been "opened" by sexual penetration it should be possible for smoke or fumes introduced into the vagina to waft upward along the "road" and emanate from her mouth or nose."

Yoni Steam

The benefits for yoni steaming are vast. Cultures across the globe and throughout history have used it to maintain female reproductive health. Modern women can do the same.

The steam regulates moon cycles for women, tones the uterus, relieves menstrual cramps, gets rid of old sludge from previous cycles, promotes fertility, helps with painful intercourse, endometriosis, ovarian cysts, supports menopause, heals post abortion or miscarriage, cleanses after toxic relationships, assists with postpartum recovery, maintains healthy vaginal flora for healthy odor, increases self appreciation, reconnects a woman to her body, and more.

When practicing at home on your own, use caution as it is hot boiling water and if you do not own a seat with a hole or one that easily goes over the toilet, you will need to activate your quads and hamstrings to squat over the bowl. Let the herbs boil (covered) and wait a few minutes till a comfortable warm temperature.

Please ensure the material of your bowl is **not** plastic as the heat of the water will leech chemicals and microplastics. It is best to use a clay, ceramic, or stainless steel.

You can use a towel or blanket to wrap around your waist to 'trap' the steam and direct it up to your yoni. It is advisable to wear a long flowy skirt or be nude from the waist down for the most comfort.

Depiction of vaginal steaming
Konark Sun Temple in Konark, India

Resensitization Practice

How do we counteract our body feeling numb and disconnected from libido, arousal, pleasure, and orgasms?

The numbness, apathy, discomfort we feel during foreplay is an indication that our body needs love and self-touch. Despite direct or indirect stimulation, the nipples stay soft, the vagina stays dry, and the clitoris remains unresponsive. There could be an unconscious clenching in the body, due to trauma or feelings of unsafety, that over time leads to numbness during intimacy.

Self-Touch Practice 

Grab organic oil like sweet almond or coconut and warm it in your hands by rubbing your palms together. With a curious mind, start massaging your inner thighs and exploring up to the vulva entrance, but not further. Repeat this practice for your chest and go slow. Cup your breasts in your hands and circle outwards, then inwards, and while deeply breathing, focus your touch on your nipple area and continue slow small circles clockwise then counterclockwise. Advanced players can incorporate crystal wands for external tummy/ovary massages and eventually G-zone exploration and sensitization. For the G-Zone, start slow and soft, perhaps using two fingers with an open, curious mind and coaxing the spongy tissue to engorge. Later incorporate toys to stimulate.

Sign up for the newsletter at wisewomb.org for future classes on these subjects.

Yoni Egg

Over 5,000 years ago, in Taoist and Ancient Chinese texts, there are references to the yoni egg as a tool reserved for empresses and concubines for the emperor in royal circles. These practices were esoteric and therefore exact facts on the origins remain murky.

Yoni Eggs, sometimes referred to as jade eggs due to their original material, are semiprecious stones carved into the shape of an egg, ranging in size from small to large, polished and meant to be inserted into the vagina. Medium size eggs are used for beginners while smaller eggs require more developed muscles and are an advanced practice. Large eggs are recommended for post childbirth or menopause.

The benefits of Yoni Eggs include increased lubrication, pleasure, strengthened and toned pelvic floor and vaginal muscles. This leads to a deeper body connection during intimacy and orgasm. Its practical uses include urinary retention and relief of PMS symptoms with regular use. *Do not use during menstruation.*

Originally these eggs were used to enhance vitality, called Qi, because inserting the egg works the pelvic muscles. In Taoist practices, sexual energy is drawn inwards and then upwards, transforming it into a refined sexual energy.

A yoni egg practice is a powerful way for females to connect with their intimate selves and cultivate a relationship with pleasure. A yoni egg will never get lost in the vagina because the cervix is a gate that only opens during menstruation and childbirth. You may not feel it inside you at first, this is normal due to the body's disconnect. With practice, more feeling will arise from the new neural pathways built to the vagina.

How to Choose Your Yoni Egg

Choose your egg wisely from a trusted source that uses high-quality crystals. Not every stone is meant to be a yoni egg. Jade, Obsidian, Rose Quartz, and Carnelian are safe choices. Trust your intuition.

Jade: Traditionally used in China. It is a healer stone meant to restore emotional balance and female reproductive vitality. A great start to the yoni egg practice.

Rose Quartz: A gentle, unconditional love stone that nourishes the soul. It is great for highly sensitive souls and beginners.

Obsidian: Meant to release deep sexual traumas and confront the shadows of your sexual self. An intermediate to advanced stone.

Carnelian: A stone of creation and cultivating your sexual energy for desire and realization into the material world. A stone for the advanced.

Other safe choices include Clear Quartz, Nephrite Jade, Amethyst. Super advanced users can work with Ben Wa Balls made of obsidian.

How to Use a Yoni Egg

Do not use during menstruation. Not recommended during pregnancy.

Step 1: Create an insertion ritual. Treat this time as special and set up candles, aromas, and soft music. Maybe sit across from a mirror.

Step 2: Place your hand over your heart and take five long, deep inhales through the nose and exhale with sound through your mouth. Place your yoni egg in between your outer labia lips and simply breathe while cupping your hand over the yoni egg and your vulva.

Step 3: Warm organic coconut oil in between your palms and massage from your inner thighs to your outer labias. Soften your belly by bringing some light touch to this area.

Step 4: It should feel like your vagina is "swallowing" your Yoni Egg. There should never be any force. Gently guide the yoni egg inside and take a moment to notice.

Step 5: There are many variations to the exercises available. Start with short 5 minute sessions and as you build strength, extend it to up to 20 minutes. Take a deep breath in and on your exhale, imagine pulling your yoni egg up to your cervix. Inhale and squeeze the egg, long hold and release on your exhale, which activates the short-twitch muscle fibers. As you breathe in a steady manner, you can perform quick pulses on the egg, which activates the fast-twitch muscle fibers. Advanced users can play with self-pleasure and sex with the egg inserted.

Yoni Egg Disclaimers

Cleansing Your Yoni Stone

In order to cleanse the yoni egg crystal from energetic baggage, consider performing frequent ritual cleanses. This can include burying the egg in salt for half an hour. Leaving it out in the sun for a few hours. Mixing a small bowl with salt and letting the egg sit out in the bowl under the sun. Bathing it in full moonlight. Burying it in the ground to recharge for 3 hours. Make sure to add a marker to remember where it is buried! Washing it in the ocean, being careful to not let the tide take it away. Placing it on top of sand or covering it in sand in a bowl. Please double check if your crystal can experience salt, water, or sunlight. Some do better with different methods.

Safety Measures

Never use your Yoni egg during your bleed and proceed with caution with any medical conditions. It is best to not use it during pregnancy although some women have continued their practice. Please use caution as the spiritual aspect of these eggs can transform sexual energy and when a woman carries life in her womb, she is directly affecting the baby. Take time to fully recover during the postpartum journey.

If you notice any nicks or cracks on your egg, do not use internally because the porous surface area can invite bacteria. There can be a burial ritual to discard it. Typically when an egg breaks, it means it has served its purpose to the user.

Wash after every use and store in a safe place.

For safety reasons, please only use eggs in the Yoni as we have a door-like mechanism with the cervix that protects it from getting lost in the body.

Sign up for the newsletter at wisewomb.org for future classes on these subjects.

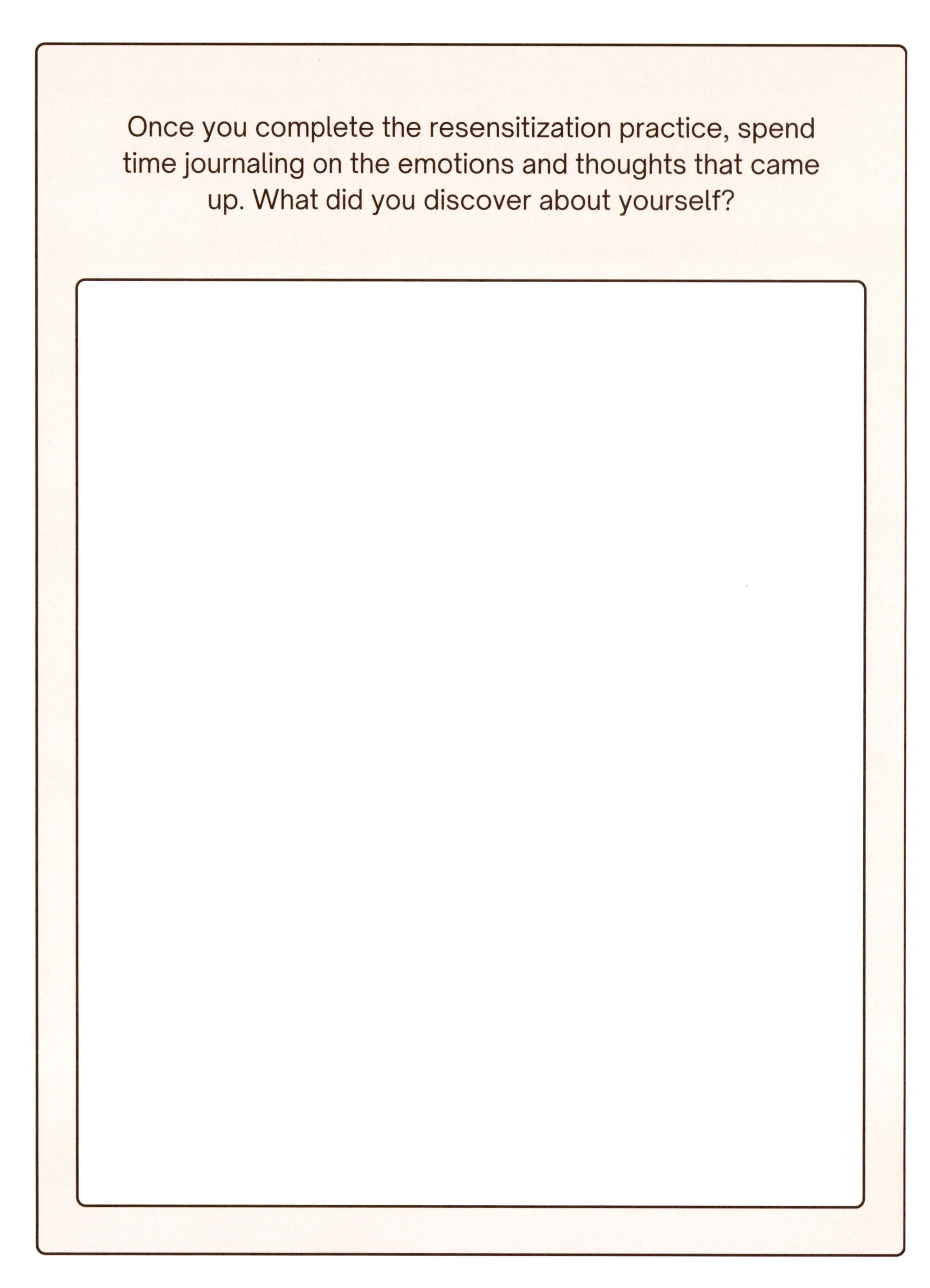
Once you complete the resensitization practice, spend time journaling on the emotions and thoughts that came up. What did you discover about yourself?

Herbal Remedies & Aphrodisiacs

Herbal Remedies

Herbs have beneficial properties for women, however, at Wise Womb, we practice bio-individuality. Listening to your body's response trumps associated benefits. Some herbs have positive effects as well as counter effects. For example, turmeric lowers inflammation but it also lowers blood sugar, which may cause the consumer to be excessively tired because of it. **Pregnant women should always proceed with caution and consult a physician to ensure safety.**

Methods of Using Herbs: Traditional and Modern Approaches

Tea

Tincture

Infusion

Essential Oil

Smoke

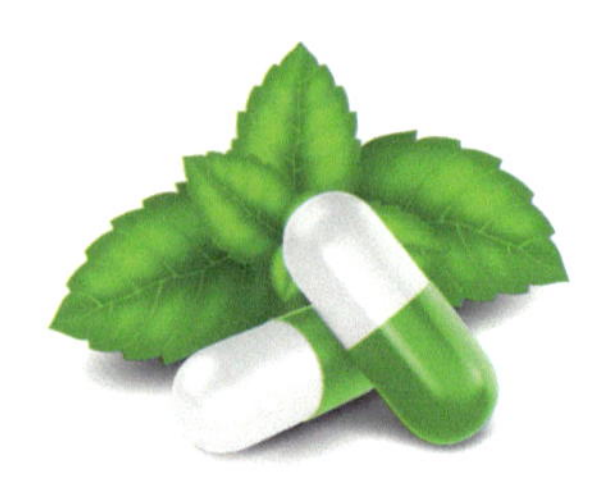

Capsule

Herbs for Women

Red Raspberry Leaf

- Strengthens and tones the uterus
- Relieves PMS symptoms and regulates cycle
- Increases blood flow to reproductive organs
- Supports pregnancy and childbirth process **caution for third trimester as it can cause premature birth. Consult a healthcare provider*

Red Clover

- Boosts fertility and eases menopause symptoms
- Anti-cancer herb due to phytosterols that are bio converted into active anti-cancer estrogens in the body
- Improves skin elasticity and heals conditions like eczema, psoriasis, rashes, acne, etc.
- Strengthens bones and teeth due to its minerals

Rose

- Uplifting flower with anti-depressant qualities

- Eases cramp severity and frequency
- Consuming rose improves sexual function
- Timeless symbol of femininity and love

This information is provided for educational purposes only and is not intended to diagnose, treat, cure, or prevent any medical condition. Always consult with a qualified healthcare professional.

Aphrodisiac Herbs

Maca

- Energizes and stimulates libido
- Supports healthy fertility
- Combats erectile dysfunction in men
- Alleviates menopausal symptoms

Blue Lotus

- Increases libido and is an aphrodisiac
- Eases cramps from menstrual cycles
- Effective natural remedy for heavy bleeding
- Psychoactive compounds that promote lucid dreams

Shatavari Root

- Supports healthy libido and sexual function
- Soothes vaginal dryness
- In Sanskrit it translates to, "She who has a hundred husbands"
- Balances hormones and boosts fertility naturally

This information is provided for educational purposes only and is not intended to diagnose, treat, cure, or prevent any medical condition. Always consult with a qualified healthcare professional.

Vulva as an Icon

Mysticism of the Feminine Body

A woman's yoni is believed to have mystical powers. Practices that revere women's genitalia dates back centuries.

"Many of these figures had pronounced breasts and *yonis*, perhaps signifying their regenerative function. Cowry shells, a common representation of the vulva, were also found at these sites. Scholars believe women most likely used these objects in rituals, perhaps together with their own menstrual and sexual fluids, in order to ensure a fruitful harvest...Numerous seals, ritual objects, and yoni/lingam structures from the later Indus Valley civilizations of Mohenjo-daro and Harappa also point to an early understanding of the sanctity of female sexuality and its association with Earth's fertility...In Kaula, Shakta, and tantric cosmogony women play a divine role due to the nature of their sex. In these ideologies libartion (Moksha) is possible to humans within this lifetime, but only through the ritual sexual practices and the worship of the *yoni*, the female sexual fluids, and the menstrual blood"

-Encyclopedia of Hinduism by Constance Jones, James D. Ryan

Cultural Significance

In many cultures of the ancient world, we find symbols and rituals honoring a woman's sacred portal. It is displayed with boldness.

Thesmorphia - Θεσμοφόρια

Thesmorphia was a three day festival in Ancient Greece, reserved for women-only, honoring Demeter Thesmorphos and her daughter, Persephone. Men were not allowed to participate or even know about the rites that occurred. The purpose of this festival was to invite divine protection for the land and secure a good harvest for the year, however customs suggest a strong acknowledgement of the feminine. While each day of the festival had its own focus, the final day honored fertility and sexuality.

Ancient evidence suggest these rituals included lewd language and crude jokes among women. In *the Return of Hephaistos, Dionysiac Procession Ritual and the Creation of a Visual Narrative*, Guy Hedreen writes, "Kleomedes compared the language employed during the Thesmophoria to that used in brothels, which suggests that the language as well as the visual symbols of the festival concerned sex." The insulting jokes were made in honor of Demeter and were seen as a celebration of the goddess rather than an attempt to be cruel. Women used insults as tool for bonding instead of exclusion. It is interesting to note how later, such as the Victorian era, women had to uphold the image of 'proper' and 'modest' while earlier generations let their wild selves embrace raunchy humor.

In *Artemis and Virginity in Ancient Greece* by Professor Pietro Vannicelli, it states, "the festival of Demeter Thesmorphos on Sicily where the goddess was offered cakes, so called "mylloi," made of sesame seed and honey in the shape of female genitals...The participants at the Thesmorphia shouted abusive words." Cakes in the shape of snakes, a timeless symbol of divine feminine and fertility, as well as vulvas were prominent. This draws onto a comparison of bachelorette parties today, with phallic symbols and party favors. The same crude humor is celebrated but within a starkly different context. In Ancient Greece, typically married citizen-wives would attend Thesmorphia and some maidens while in modern day culture, this practice is societally acceptable for maidens in 'pre-marriage' celebrations, not after.

Ana Suromai

The gesture of 'ana suromai' or 'anasyrma' directly translates from Greek and means "to lift up your skirt." It is found in many cultures; exposing a female's genitalia was associated with mystical powers to enhance fertility and ward off evil spirits.

Cross Culture Phenomenon

In mythology, groups of women would defeat gods by raising their skirts. In Celtic culture, the Irish sun god Cú Chulainn and in Greek it was Bellerophon who were defeated. The custom was practiced during the Thesmorphos festival as well as the Ancient Egyptian Bubastis for increasing fertility. In Japan there is a myth of an angered sun goddss Amaterasu-o-mi-Kame, another goddess Ame-no-uzume coaxed Amaterasu out of her cave through a dance exposing her breasts and genitals. A strong theme persists throughout different cultures, which is exposing genitals and laughter brings about fertility, prosperity, and protection.

Isis statue from Ancient Greece with a proud woman in a full length dress and headdress lifting her skirt for all to see.

In Milan at Porta Tosa, a statue of a woman raising her skirt. She protects the city.

Ana Suromai Depictions

Even today, at the Kanshoji Temple in Tatebayashi, Japan there is a sacred yoni symbol that worshippers go to touch. There are no images available of it online.

Syrian seal showing goddess lifting her skirt to expose her vulva.

Isis statue from 1 BCE in Egypt

Baubò Statue from Italy

Ana Suromai

By Amanda Sage

Sumer

Sumer is a civilization in Mesopotamia that existed over 7,000 years ago. Female sexuality was worshipped in the Sumerian religion.

As Catherine Faurot states in the article, *The Secret History of the Vulva,* "In one of the earliest hymns, the goddess Inanna celebrates the beauty of her genitals: 'When Inanna leaned against the apple tree, her vulva was wondrous to behold. Rejoicing at her wondrous vulva, the young woman applauded herself…' The high priestess, representing Inanna, is seated on a throne, while the king, representing her consort, approaches. The liturgy reads: "The king goes with lifted head to the holy vulva / He goes with lifted head to the holy vulva of Inanna…." These rites were part of a seven-day long new year's festival, which opened with the high priestess and king having sex and concluded with orgies meant to stimulate the fertility of the land, animals and humans." The Sumerian civilization, with a religion starkly different to our monotheistic religions, has endured longer than Christianity.

Even though the modern day religions, Christianity, Judaism, Islam, do not overtly honor the Goddess archetype or explicitly revere the vulva, her presence remains solid. Faurot includes the below examples in her article:

- The vulva of the Hebrew goddess was represented by a pit or pool of water in the heart of ancient Jewish temples.

- The Kaaba, the black stone at the center of the Islamic pilgrimage, was originally sacred to a goddess known as Al'Lat and is now enshrined in a silver vulva, which pilgrims ceremoniously touch.

- In Christianity, the vulva appears as a radiant oval, representative of cosmic creation, surrounding either Jesus Christ or the Virgin Mary. This yonic form is ubiquitous in Christian art, appearing as a flat oval in art and as a three-dimensional oval niche surrounding statues of sacred figures.

Inanna & Ishtar

While Sumerians had Inanna, Mesopotamia worshipped Ishtar, a goddess representing love and fertility. Both are said to refer to the same diety. The language is explicit and reveres the feminine body and its powers.

In *L'érotisme sacré* by Jean Bottéro, Ishtar says to her lover:

Who will plow my high field?
Who will plow my wet ground?
As for me, the young woman,
who will plow my vulva?
Who will station the ox there?

According to the myth of Inanna and Dumuzi,

Dumuzi replied:
—*Great Lady, the king will plow your vulva.*
I, Dumuzi the King, will plow your vulva.

Inanna:
—*Then plow my vulva, man of my heart!*
Plow my vulva!

"When she leaned against the apple tree, her vulva was wondrous to behold...rejoicing at her wondrous vulva, the young woman Inanna applauded herself."

"Like her mouth, her vulva is sweet" (Alster 1985: 133)

Ishtar, vase from Larsa, c. 1900 BC. Musée du Louvre

Symbolism

The vulva has been an inspiration throughout cultures and expresses itself in architecture and statues. It mirrors itself in the human body.

"Her lap is the holy altar, her hair, the sacred grass; the lips of her Yoni are the fire in the middle."
-Brhad Aranyika Upanishad

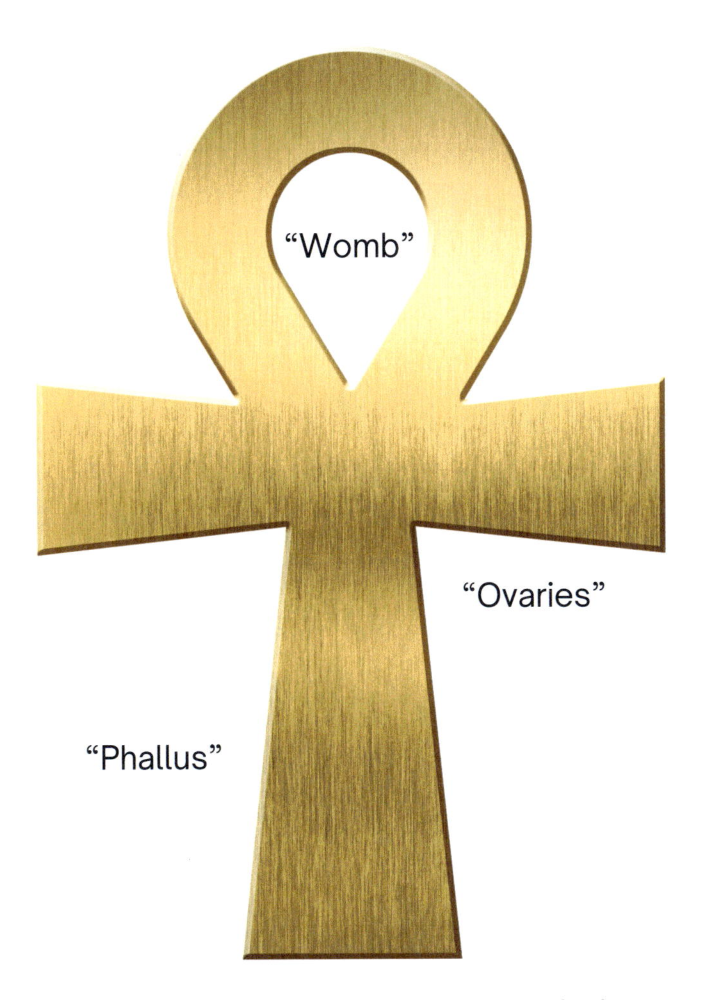

'Ankh" an Ancient Egyptian symbol

Great Door of Amiens Cathedral

Vesica Piscis

Vesica Piscis translates to the “vessel of the fish.” In ancient cultures, it represents the womb. In Italian, it is called a ‘mandorla’ or almond because of its shape. In Greek it is called ‘Ichthys,’ believed to be the child of the Syrian Goddess Atargatis. This symbol has been honored as the ‘Great Mother’ and the portal of life.

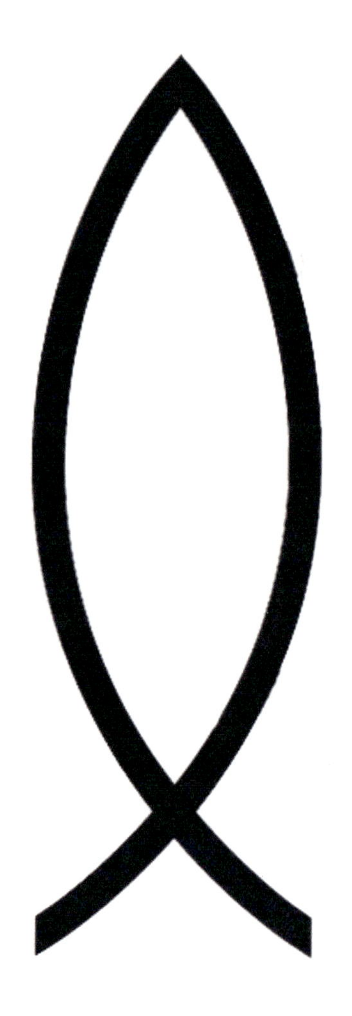

Vesica Piscis

The Cosmic Egg
Hildegard of Bingen (1098-1179)

Sheela-na-gig

In England, Ireland, France, and more between the 12th and 17th century, Sheela-na-gigs prominently adorned Catholic churches at keystone positions above its arch entrances. Similar figures are found in an island in Oceana.

"Aside from the transformative religious mysteries of sacrifice and initiation, the obvious life-giving and growth-promoting powers of the vulva and its secretions have given rise to a widespread use of representations of the female genitalia as apotropaic devices. The custom of plowing a furrow for magical protection around a town was practiced all over Europe by peasants. It was still observed in the twentieth century in Russia, where villages were thus annually 'purified.' The practice was exclusively carried out by women, who, while plowing, called on the moon goddess. A similar apotropaic function seems to have prompted the placing of squatting female figures prominently exposing their open vulvas on the key of arches at church entrances in Ireland, Great Britain, and German Switzerland. In Ireland these figures are called Sheelagh-na-gigs. Some of these figures represent emaciated old women. These images are illustrations of myths concerning the territorial Celtic goddess who was the granter of royalty. When the goddess wished to test the king-elect, she came to him in the form of an old hag, soliciting sexual intercourse. If the king-elect accepted, she transformed herself into a radiantly beautiful young woman and conferred on him royalty and blessed his reign. Most such figures were removed from churches in the nineteenth century.

...

A remarkable parallel to the Celtic Sheelagh-na-gig is found in the Palauan archipelago. The wooden figure of a nude woman, prominently exposing her vulva by sitting with legs wide apart and extended to either side of the body, is placed on the eastern gable of each village's chiefly meeting house. Such figures are called dilugai. Interestingly, the yoni [the female genitalia] is in the shape of a cleft downward-pointing triangle. These female figures protect the villagers' health and ward off all evil spirits as well. They are constructed by ritual specialists according to strict rules, which if broken would result in the specialist's as well as the chiefs death. It is not coincidental that each example of signs representing the female genitalia used as apotropaic devices are found on gates. The vulva is the primordial gate, the mysterious divide between nonlife and life" (Encyclopedia of Religion, article YONI, Vol.15, p.534)

Representations

A sheela na gig carving at the Watergate in Fethard, Co Tipperary.
Photograph: Maurice Savage/Alamy

The Oaksey in Wiltshire
from Sheela Na Gig Project

Sheela Na Gig in Kilpeck
Church, UK.

Representations

Dilukai from the Caroline Islands in Palau

Rahara, Ireland photographed by Gabriel Cannon

Project Sheela

“Project Sheela is a street art project founded by two Irish artists to celebrate, commemorate and commiserate with the history of women's rights in Ireland. Project Sheela places handmade ceramic sheela na gigs at new locations each year for Women’s Day in Ireland & international locations.

...

Project Sheela hopes to heal some of those wounds and to promote an attitude towards women and their sexuality that is positive and empowering. Each year the project raises money for important women's charities by selling a limited number of handmade sheelas.”

ProjectSheela.com

Wall of a Thousand Vulvas

In Queensland, Australia there is an Aboriginal rock stencil art site called Carnarvon Gorge that lacks world recognition. There are up to a thousand vulvas etched into the wall. At one site, the description is called *A Woman's Story* and reads, "Women are responsible for looking after some of the stories etched along this section of the sandstone wall – women's business. You will see engraved over and over again the motif of the human vulva. Our Elders tell the story of this design being a fertility symbol." The wall should be protected as a sacred feminine site.

Photo by Glenys D. Livingstone in *Goddess Pilgrimage Central Queensland Australia* in Mago Magazine

Photo: Don Hitchcock, donsmaps.com

Pilgrim Vulva

In medieval Europe, people carried talismans in the image of a vulva dressed as a pilgrim on the Camino de Santiago, a pilgrimage to the Cathedral of Santiago de Compostela in Galicia, Spain.

These pilgrimage badges depicting a “Wandering Woman” archetype have been found scattered along river banks next to traditional religious badges, suggesting that religion embraced sexuality. The Pilgrim’s Guide writes, “These profane badges were produced across the fourteenth through sixteenth centuries. Despite being worn on these innately religious pilgrimages, in museum collections they are labeled secular but stored alongside the “holy” badges. The ‘semantic choice in labeling badges with sexual content as profane and cataloging them alongside sacred pilgrim badges implies that the two types are linked, albeit oppositional.’”

Jos Koldeweij in his work writes,“In Rotterdam a fragment showing phallic creatures bearing a stretcher was found, in Bruges a complete example of a variant: a brooch consisting of three phalluses carrying a crowned vulva on a bier. The association with a religious procession will have been evident to everyone of that period who saw the brooch.”

Reproduction of ‘Procession of three phallic figures carrying crowned vulva on a litter’ found in Bruges, Belgium 1375-1424.

Image from Etsy sellers who create replicas of these badges

Replicas and Originals

Pilgrim Vulva photo from Universidad de los Andes

Photo from Parody and Satire in Early Modern Spain by Frank Dominguez

Photo from Jos Koldeweij in "Shameless and Naked Images"

Replica from the 14th century of a Queen Pilgrim Vulva from The Pilgrim's Guide

Etymology of 'Cunt'

The word 'cunt' strikes controversy in the modern world; it is reserved as a severe insult and most who use profanity never utter the 'c' word. However, the etymology of the word 'cunt' gives us a clue to a deeper history.

Goddesses

The oriental Goddess Cunti, also known as Kunda, was referred to as 'Yoni of the Universe.' Yoni, as shared previously, means vulva. In Hindu mythology, there is a main character whose name is Kunti; she was a queen in the Mahabharata. The Greeks had a goddess named 'Kunthus.' The Romans had a goddess named "Cunina" who protects newborns in the cradle. Her sister, "Cuba" protects children and is said to protect the transition from the cradle to bed. Cundi, meaning "Supreme Purity," is a Buddhist deity with spelling variations in the Chinese and Japanese cultures. According to the Enlightenment Thangka, she is the mother of all deities in the Lotus class.

High Priestess

The Canaanites inhabited Ancient Near East, called the Levant, sometimes referred to as Palestine, where today parts of Israel, Jordan, and Syria exist. The Canaanites had a term for the high priestess, 'Khnt,' which indicates that women led spiritual rituals in their culture. This is distinct from Jewish and Catholic religions, where rabbinism and priesthood are reserved for men.

In *The Mother of Eshmunazor, Priest of Astarte: A Study of her Cultic Role* by Susan Ackerman she writes, "Other instances of women identified as priestesses, or *khnt*, in Phoenician tradition...for example, a grave inscription from Avignon that...describes its honorand as a *khnt* of a goddess who is called *rbt*, or "The Great Lady" (line 1)... A similar gravestone from Djebel Mansour, in modern-day Tunisia (*KAI* 140), has carved upon its bilingual inscription in Neo-Punic and Latin that also describes its honorand as a priestess (using the Neo-Punic spelling *knt*; line 2).This inscription further describes the priestess as responsible for building the temple...Other *khnt* are found on grave inscriptions from Carthage; these include, most remarkably, the grave inscription of Batba'al, the 'head' (*rb*) of the *khnm*, and the two separate grave inscriptions of Hld and Hnb'l, who are both memorialized in their epitaphs as *rb khnt*, or the 'chief priestess.'"

Reflective Journaling Pages

Do you see the mirroring between your Throat & Yoni?

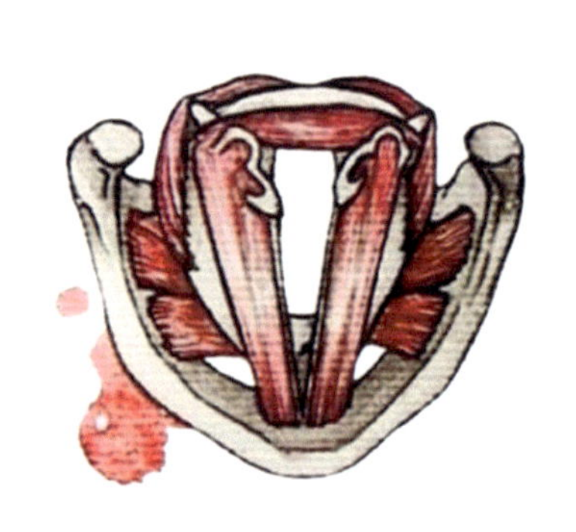

Vocal Cords

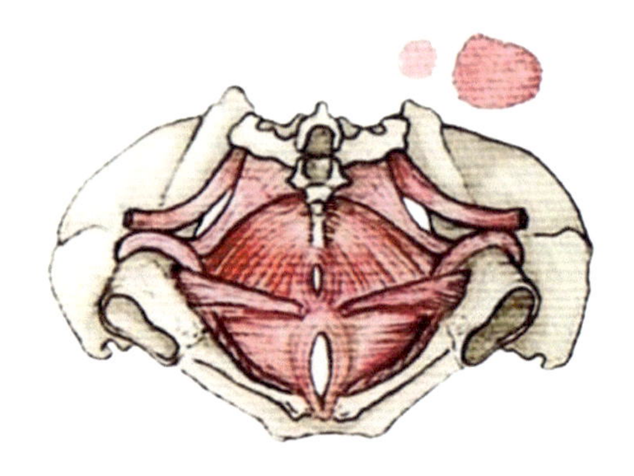

Pelvic Floor

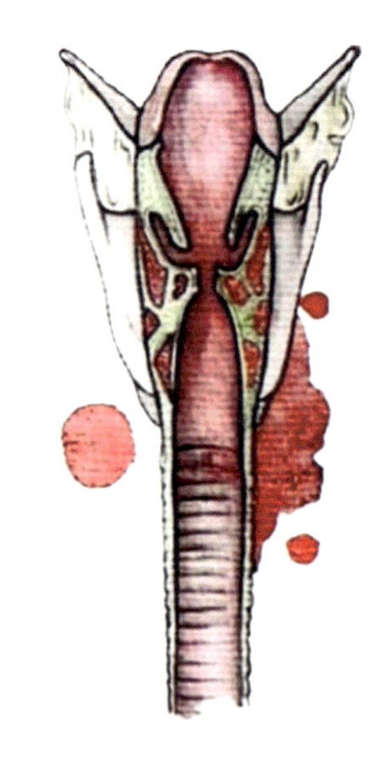

Larynx

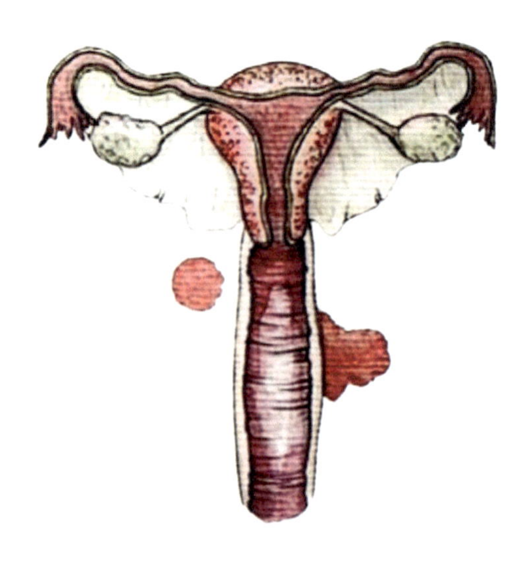

Uterus

Art by Luisa Alexandre

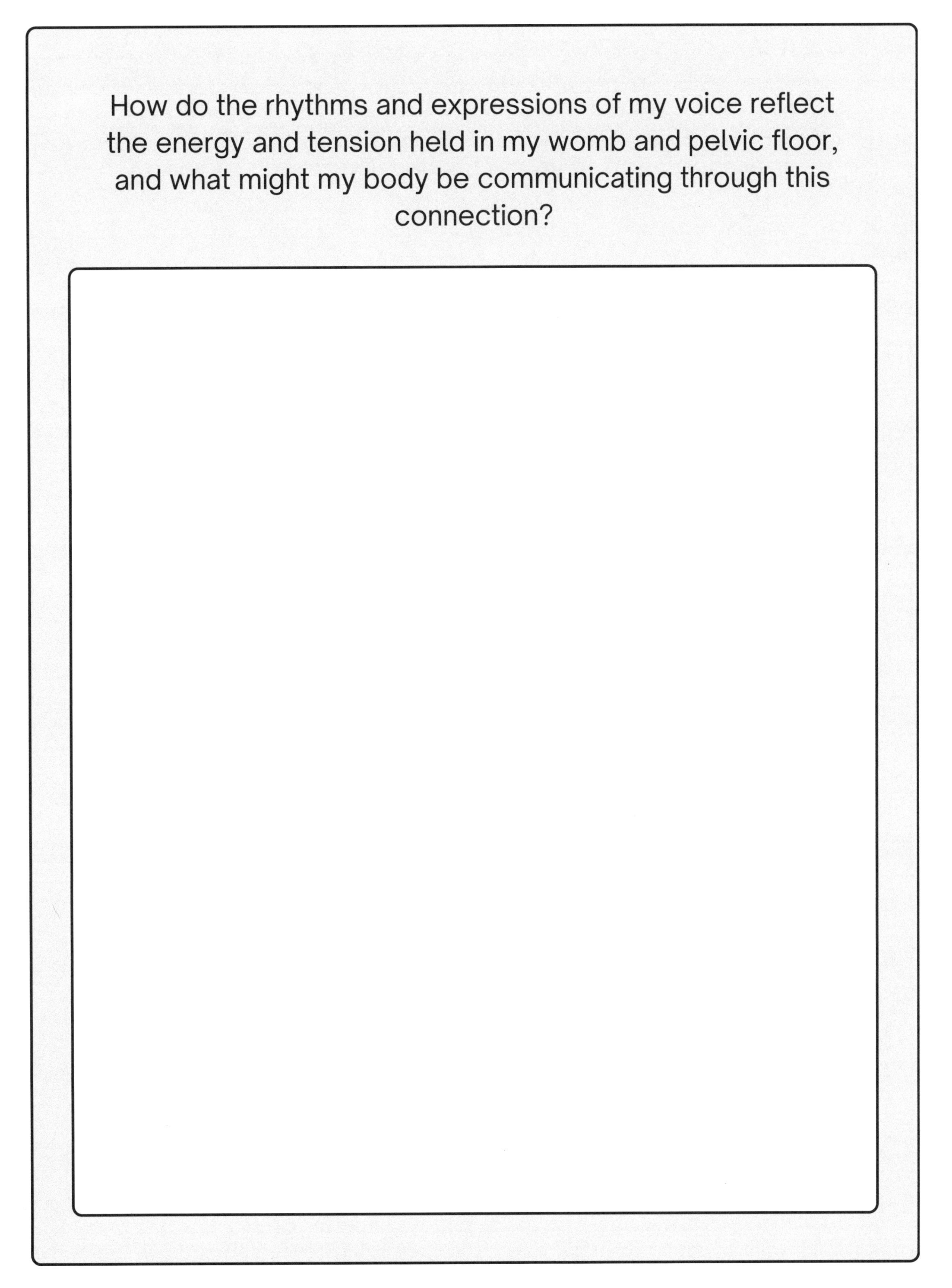
How do the rhythms and expressions of my voice reflect the energy and tension held in my womb and pelvic floor, and what might my body be communicating through this connection?

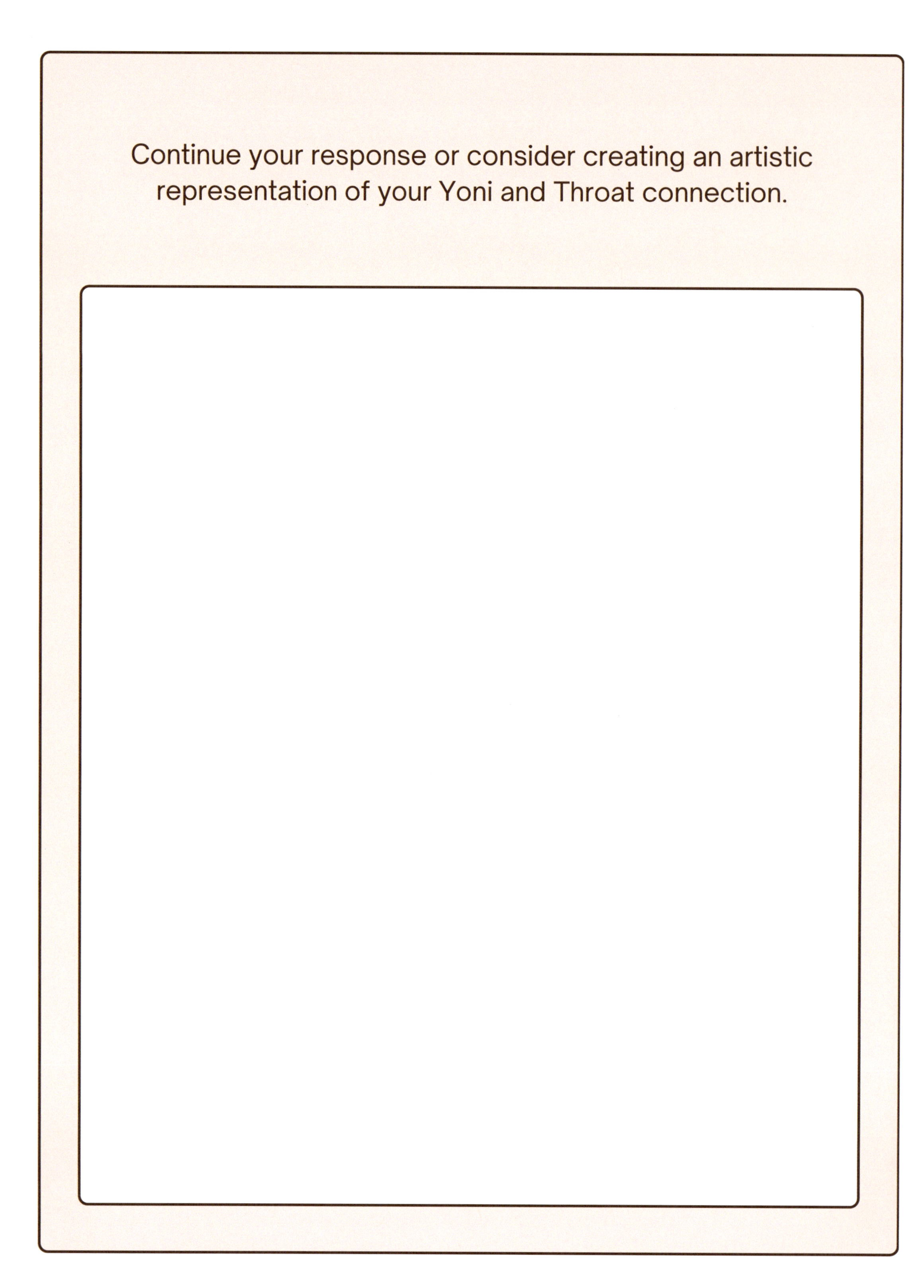

Continue your response or consider creating an artistic representation of your Yoni and Throat connection.

What is your relationship to arousal? Can you identify how your body responds when you feel hot?

Celebrate Yourself!

What have you learned in this workbook?

How will I celebrate myself for honoring my womanhood and taking the time to learn about my incredible body?

Founders of
Wise Womb Foundation

Founder's Highlight

Olivia Dzumaga

Sacred Intimacy Mentor

Olivia is a Sacred Intimacy Mentor who educates females how to embrace their sensuality. She believes in monogamous relationships and is passionate about teaching women how to blend spirituality with intimacy. She has studied Integrated Energy Therapy, Akashic records, and Erotic Blueprints. She examines primary sources to educate women on the history of sex and feminism. Her perspective on sexuality is shaped by her personal study of works by Kinsey, Dr. Money, Dr. Reisman, and others.

Olivia grew up in Queens, NY and is a dancer since childhood; she started as a ballerina. At the age of 6, she took a summer course on belly dancing. Fifteen years later, she devoted herself to learning Raqs Sharqi and Raqs Magrhibi, while exploring other dance styles. Olivia combines her interest in esoteric knowledge and mysticism to transform dance into a healing modality for herself and clients. She works 1:1 with women online and in NYC to own their sensual nature.

For pricing & details visit WiseWomb.org

Founder's Highlight

Julie Fotis

Intuitive Womanhood

Julie Fotis is a certified Holistic Health coach, as well as a certified Holistic Pregnancy and Birth practitioner and has been supporting men and women to heal and break free from subconscious, transgenerational trauma and self-sabotaging patterns.

Julie is a French mama of two boys and has found New York City to be her new home since 2012. Her whole healing journey created an undeniable passion for Birth Justice, Female Health Justice and overall humanity's well-being. After working for seven years as an energy healer and birth educator, she is thrilled to create content for the preventive and educational platform that Wise Womb offers and take the sponsorship of doulas for mamas-in-need as a life mission.

She offers a wide range of services from 1:1 Soul Healing sessions to Holistic Birth Preparation in a hospital set up and leads meditations for each class offered through the Wise Womb Foundation.

For pricing & details visit WiseWomb.org

Founder's Highlight

Adelemarie Palermo

Renaissance Magazine

Adelemarie is an advocate for cycle awareness and female nourishment. Her struggle with painful periods during her teen years led her on a journey of cycle awareness, transforming not only how she viewed her body but also how she saw herself. Through learning more about her body and finding ways to support it, she experienced reduced period pain along with increased confidence and vitality. Embracing her feminine self inspired her to create Renaissance Woman Magazine, a digital writing platform where she shares her passion for learning, art, and culture with her readers. Born from a childhood feeling of being a "jack of all trades, master of none," her goal is to encourage the natural curiosity, creativity, and intellectualism of her audience, proving that anyone can be their own muse. She brings this same zeal to Wise Womb, aiming to inspire women to embrace their instinctive cyclical nature and creative power.

For details visit WiseWomb.org

Bibliography

Ackerman, Susan. "The Mother of Eshmunazor, Priest of Astarte: A Study of Her Cultic Role." Die Welt Des Orients 43, no. 2 (2013): 158–78. http://www.jstor.org/stable/23608853.

Alessia Beretta, Valentina. The Anasyrma Fertility Ritual in Ancient Egypt: From Hathor to Hermaphroditus. Birmingham Egyptology Journal, 2024, 10, pp.22-35. ffhal-04447049f.

Arvigo, Rosita. "Vaginal Steams: Forgotten Ancient Wisdom for Women's Healing." Birth Institute. https://www.birth-institute.com/alternative-medicine-and-childbirth/vaginal-steams.

Blackledge, Catherine. "Raise the Skirt, Reclaim Your Power." Catherine Blackledge, 2020. http://catherineblackledge.com/raise-the-skirt-reclaim-your-power/.

Blank, Hanne. "A Pot of Herbs, A Plastic Sheet, and Thou: A Historian Goes for a 'V-Steam.'" Nursing Clio, August 4, 2015. https://nursingclio.org/2015/08/04/a-pot-of-herbs-a-plastic-sheet-and-thou-a-historian-goes-for-a-v-steam/.

Bottéro, Jean, and Samuel Noah Kramer. L'érotisme sacré. Paris: Univers Poche, 2014.
Carter, Jasmine Alicia. "Yoni Egg: The Hidden Secret from Ancient China's Royal Palace." Sacred Woman, June 23, 2021.

Catherine, Faurot. "A Brief History of the Vulva in Art." Ms. Magazine, March 25, 2023. https://msmagazine.com/2023/03/25/vulva-art-history/.

Coleman, Meghan. "Yoni Steaming." Sage Birth & Wellness Collective, March 27, 2020. https://sagebirthandwellness.com/2020/03/yoni-steaming-by-meghan-coleman/#:~:text=Yoni%20steaming%20is%20the%20practice,the%20menstrual%20cycle%20is%20done.

Collings, Trudy. "Yoni Steaming: The Ancient Self-Care Practice for Loving Your Vagina." Paavani Ayurveda, May 13, 2022. https://paavaniayurveda.com/blogs/the-ayurvedic-lifestyle/yoni-steaming-the-ancient-self-care-practice-for-loving-your-vagina?srsltid=AfmBOorvrRjC_DtrEdl0pghdhqgeU8RnAhYnZDinACxsFIY3IsyIKDox.

Dickson, Keith. "Inanna." Purdue University. https://web.ics.purdue.edu/~kdickson/inanna.html.
Esa. "Gynecology." Lady Esa. https://ladyesa.wordpress.com/gynecology/.

Goode, Starr. "Icon of a Vulva." In Archeomythology, vol. 10 (2021). Institute of Archeomythology. https://www.starrgoode.com/PDFs/GoodeArcheomythology.pdf.

Green, Monica H., ed. and trans. The Trotula: A Medieval Compendium of Women's Medicine. The Middle Ages Series. Philadelphia: University of Pennsylvania Press, 2001.

Hedreen, Guy. The Return of Hephaistos, Dionysiac Procession Ritual and the Creation of a Visual Narrative. Ann Arbor: University of Michigan Press, 2004.

Hinds, Sarah. "Late Medieval Sexual Badges as Sexual Signifiers." Medieval Feminist Forum 55, no. 2 (2020): 170–191. https://doi.org/10.17077/1536-8742.2224.

Hinds, Sarah. "Late Medieval Sexual Badges as Sexual Signifiers." Medieval Feminist Forum 55, no. 2 (2020): 170–191. https://scholarworks.wmich.edu/cgi/viewcontent.cgi?article=2224&context=mff.

Hume, Robert Ernest, trans. Brihadâranyaka Upanishad. Oxford: Oxford University Press, 1921.

Jones, Constance, and James D. Ryan. Encyclopedia of Hinduism. New York: Facts On File, 2007.

Koldeweij, Jos. "Shameless and Naked Images: Obscene Badges as Parodies of Popular Devotion." In Art and Architecture of Late Medieval Pilgrimage in Northern Europe and the British Isles, edited by Rita Tekippe and Sarah Blick. Boston and Leiden: Brill, 2005.

Leick, Gwendolyn. Sex and Eroticism in Mesopotamian Literature. London: Routledge, 1994.
Riddle, John M. Goddesses, Elixirs, and Witches: Plants and Sexuality throughout Human History. New York: Palgrave Macmillan US, 2010.

Rodriguez, Marie. "The Mayan Yoni Steam." Dr. Marie Rodriguez, June 13, 2017. https://drmarierodriguez.com/2017/06/13/the-mayan-yoni-steam/.

Sage, Amanda. "Ana Suromai." Visionary Art, 2019. https://visionary.art/interviews/ana-suromai-by-amanda-sage/.

Schnur, Susan. "From Prehistoric Cave Art to Your Cookie Pan: Tracing the Hamantasch Herstory." Lilith Magazine, March 14, 1998.

Sissa, Giulia. Greek Virginity. Cambridge: Harvard University Press, 1990.
Tsubaki Grand Shrine of America. "Ame-No-Uzume-No-Mikoto." Tsubaki Grand Shrine of America. https://tsubakishrine.org/history/ame-no-uzume-no-mikoto.html.

"The Erotic Language of Carajicomedia." In Carajicomedia: Parody and Satire in Early Modern Spain, edited by Frank A. Domínguez and Bruce R. Burningham, page range. Woodbridge, UK: Tamesis, 2014.

"The Vulva Goes on Pilgrimage." Wonders & Marvels, May 2012. https://www.wondersandmarvels.com/2012/05/the-vulva-goes-on-pilgrimage.html.

Thea, Anna. "Yoni Egg History & Why This Ancient Practice Is Good for Women's Sexual Health." Medium, April 20, 2020.

Vakkas, Christina. "The Thesmophoria: Women's Ritual in the Ancient World." Hellenic Museum, October 26, 2022.

Vannicelli, Pietro. "Artemis and Virginity in Ancient Greece."
"Yoni." In Encyclopedia of Religion, edited by Mircea Eliade, Vol. 15, p. 534. New York: Macmillan, 1987.

Multiple photos are sourced from Wiki Commons and public databases.

Love the content? Snap a pic and tag us @Wise_Womb_NYC

Send a copy to your girlfriends as a gift!

Made in the USA
Columbia, SC
16 April 2025

56538088R00044